© Carole Marsh/Gallopade International • www.gallopade.com • It's Your World: United Kingdom

Live • Work • Play • Learn

GALLOPADE INTERNATIONAL

©2009 Carole Marsh/Gallopade International

Permission is hereby granted to the individual purchaser or classroom teacher to reproduce materials in this book for non-commercial, individual, or classroom use only. Reproduction of these materials for an entire school or school system is strictly prohibited.

Gallopade International is introducing SAT words that kids need to know in our books. The SAT words in this book have a gray box around them. Students can look up the definitions and increase their vocabulary. Happy Learning!

Gallopade is proud to be a member and supporter of these educational organizations and associations:

Association for the Study of African American Life and History
National Alliance of Black School Educators
American Booksellers Association
American Library Association
International Reading Association
National Association for Gifted Children
The National School Supply and Equipment Association
The National Council for the Social Studies
Museum Store Association
Association of Partners for Public Lands
Association of Booksellers for Children

At the time of publication, all websites referenced in this document were valid. However, due to the changing nature of the Internet, some addresses may change or the content become less relevant.

It's Your World Books

Africa: A Safari Through Its Amazing Nations!

Australia: The Land Down Under for Mates of All Ages!

Canada: The Maple Leaf Melting Pot Country!

China: A Great Wall Runs Thru It!

Egypt: An Ancient Land of Lore; a Modern Land of Oil and More!

France: The Ooh-La-La Country Everyone Loves!

Germany: The Country of Fairytale Castles and Cutting Edge Science!

Greece: A Volcanic Land of Ancient Olympic Origins!

India: Land of Six Senses and Intriguing Mystery!

Italy: The Country of Amazing Fountains and Awesome Arts!

Japan: An Island Country of Endless Intrigue!

Mexico: A Colorful Land of Exotic Culture!

Middle East: Ancient Countries of Current Events Headlines!

Russia: The Great Bear and Its Dramatic History!

South America: A Continent of Countries of Amazing Proportions!

United Kingdom: The Country of Ships, Sealing Wax, Cabbages, and Kings!

Other Carole Marsh Related Titles:

The Mystery at Big Ben

Table of Contents

© Carole Marsh/Gallopade International • www.gallopade.com • It's Your World: United Kingdom

A Letter from the Author

From the desk of CAROLE MARSH

Hey kids,

It's your world! It really, really is! Of course, you already know that, don't you? You surf the 'net, listen to satellite radio, watch television shows and movies set all around the globe–kids today are much more "worldly" than in the past and that's a good thing!

Now's a great time to learn something about another country–such as the United Kingdom. Why? Because one day, you might actually visit there (if you have not already!). You might go to school there–many colleges have ties with international schools around the globe. You might even go on to work in a foreign country!

Many companies have positions in other countries. Companies are "going global" as fast as they can. They have branch offices, manufacturing plants, and customer service centers scattered around the globe!

So, ready or not: YOU are a Citizen of the World! And you'll want to be a good one. How do you do that? You'll find out everything you can about that country, how it's the same, and how it's different from your own country. What language is spoken there? What customs do the people observe? What foods do they enjoy? What do they do for fun? What has happened in this part of the world and what is happening there now? It's fun ... and the more you learn the more you will enjoy whatever global opportunity comes your way!

This book is a good place to start your learning journey–so take advantage of the world– IT'S YOUR WORLD after all ... and guess what? It's a BIG world, after all!

Happy traveling and learning,

Carole Marsh
Always with passport in hand!

Why Should We Care About the United Kingdom?

The United Kingdom is made up of England, Wales, Scotland, and Northern Ireland. This cluster of islands has played a remarkable role in the history of the world! The variety and sense of history here makes it popular with tourists from around the globe. You can "see" history at many ancient sites. The United Kingdom is a land of castles, royalty, Roman baths, Stonehenge, the Tower of London, Loch Ness, and so much more!

The Industrial Revolution began here. Today, the United Kingdom's people continue to be pioneers of industry and in the idea that people can change their society. The arts thrive here—theatre, museums, and literature. And the food is as varied as the countryside!

One day, you might visit the United Kingdom to see a play, attend college at Oxford or Cambridge, live in an apartment in London, vacation at Brighton Beach, or stay in a castle. It could happen!

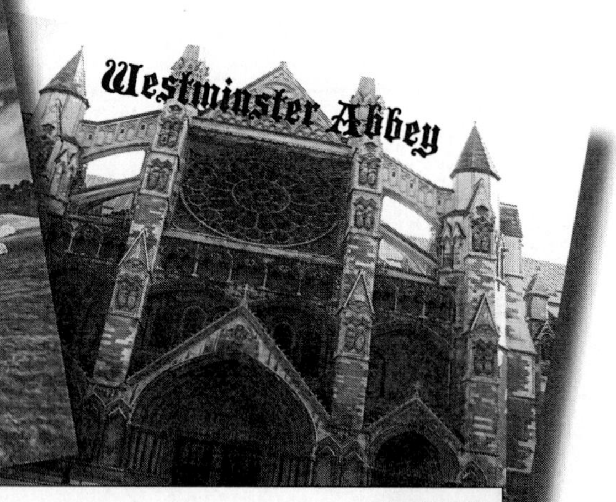

Write home about it!
What will your postcard from the United Kingdom say?

© Carole Marsh/Gallopade International • www.gallopade.com • It's Your World: United Kingdom

Top Fast United Kingdom Facts!

Important facts to remember about the United Kingdom:

- The United Kingdom is officially called the United Kingdom of Great Britain and Northern Ireland.
- The head of government in the United Kingdom is the prime minister.
- The United Kingdom is governed by a constitutional monarchy.
- Today, the United Kingdom is home to immigrants from many nations.
- The United Kingdom is a founding member of the United Nations and a member of the European Union.
- The United Kingdom has the second largest economy in Europe.
- The United Kingdom has 31 million visitors a year.
- The capital of the United Kingdom is London.
- London is a major world financial center.
- The United Kingdom's currency is the pound sterling.
- The official language is English.
- The United Kingdom's major resources are coal, oil, and natural gas.
- There is no place in the United Kingdom that is more than 62 miles from the sea!

Now, you figure out the rest!

1. This is the United Kingdom's ___ ___ ___ ___.
2. The head of state is the ___ ___ ___ ___ ___.
3. The U.K. is a cluster of ___ ___ ___ ___ ___ ___ ___.
4. The ___ ___ ___ ___ ___ ___ ___ ___ name of the United Kingdom is the United Kingdom of Great Britain and Northern Ireland.
5. The ___ ___ ___ ___ ___ ___ ___ ___ ___ ___ of the United Kingdom is about 60 million people.
6. England, Wales, Scotland and Northern Ireland make up the ___ ___ ___ ___ ___ ___ ___ ___ ___ ___ ___ ___ ___ ___.

© Carole Marsh/Gallopade International • www.gallopade.com • It's Your World: United Kingdom

Where in the World Is the United Kingdom?

- The United Kingdom is in Western Europe.
- The United Kingdom is often called Great Britain and consists of England, Scotland, Wales, and Northern Ireland.
- London is the capital city, located in southern England.
- Important bodies of water include the Irish Sea, the Atlantic Ocean, the North Sea, and the Thames River.
- The United Kingdom is an island nation.
- The climate is often windy, cloudy, and rainy. Bring your umbrella!
- The United Kingdom is about half the size of France.
- Ben Nevis in Scotland is the highest peak in the United Kingdom.
- The United Kingdom has some large forests: Kielder Forest in Northumberland; the New Forest in Hampshire; and others in Wales and Scotland.

Do You Know?

1. The United Kingdom is often called:
   a. Scotland b. Wales c. Ireland d. Great Britain

2. The United Kingdom is located in:
   a. Africa b. India c. North America d. Western Europe

© Carole Marsh/Gallopade International • www.gallopade.com • It's Your World: United Kingdom

In the Beginning...

Did you know that people lived in England more than 8,000 years ago? The population expanded when a large wave of people arrived from Europe around 4500 B.C.E. These early settlers raised livestock and farmed. They may also have built great stone structures like Stonehenge.

The Romans conquered England in the first century C.E. The Romans built forts and roads. They introduced Christianity to the region. England grew and prospered for 400 years under Roman rule. The Romans eventually left, and several invaders, including the Anglo-Saxons and the Vikings, attacked England.

The Anglo-Saxons were a Germanic tribe. The Normans, a French people, eventually overthrew them. Normans and Anglo-Saxons fought each other. Eventually their customs and language blended into present-day England.

Crosswords!

Use your new knowledge to fill in the crossword puzzle.

Across

2. People have lived in __________ for 8,000 years.
4. England was conquered by the __________ in the first century.
5. Anglo-Saxons are a __________ tribe.

Down

1. England was attacked by Anglo-Saxons and __________.
3. __________ are a French people.

© Carole Marsh/Gallopade International • www.gallopade.com • It's Your World: United Kingdom

The Amazing History of the United Kingdom!

The United Kingdom has a long and dramatic history of invasions, kings and queens, and economic prosperity and prestige. The British Empire was once the largest in history. It included almost one fourth of the world's land and one fifth of its people. The British navy ruled the seas.

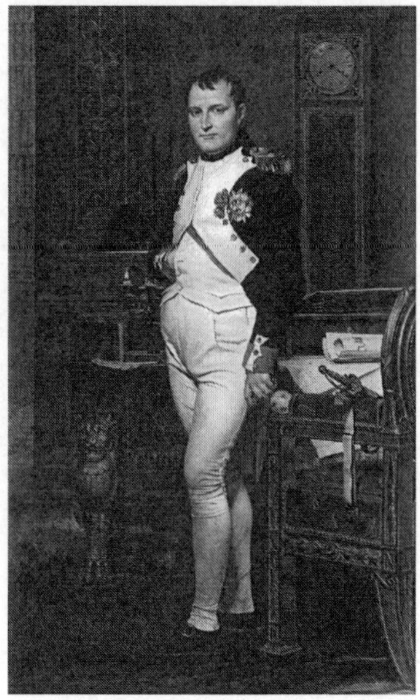
Napoleon Bonaparte

During the Hundred Years' War from 1337 to 1453, England fought with its neighbor, France. Before the war was over, the black plague killed 40 percent of the people in England! Territories in North America, the island of Bermuda, and a few islands in the Caribbean were added to the British Empire starting in the 1600s. In 1793, France declared war on Great Britain once again. The two countries signed a treaty in 1801. In 1815, Great Britain joined the fight to defeat France's emperor Napoleon Bonaparte. The British victory against Napoleon at Waterloo in June 1815 made Britain the dominant power in Europe.

Great Britain once again went to war in the 1900s. Prime Minister Winston Churchill emerged a leader and hero during World War I (1914-1918) and World War II (1939-1945).

Today, like many developed countries, the United Kingdom struggles with economic issues, the war on terrorism, immigration, health care, climate change, and other modern problems. In the meantime, it remains a beautiful country with hopes for a great future!

Timeline!
Number these events in the order that they took place, first to last.

______ The British fight in World War I.

______ England fights with its neighbor, France.

______ Winston Churchill is a hero.

______ Britain is the dominant power in Europe.

______ The British fight in World War II.

______ Black plague kills 40 percent of the English people.

© Carole Marsh/Gallopade International • www.gallopade.com • It's Your World: United Kingdom

Famous English Folks

Matching!

Match these famous English folks with their accomplishments.

1. _____ I joined the British army in 1895 and was elected to Parliament in 1900. I was called both a hero and warmonger during WWI and WWII. I served under four kings and resigned as prime minister of Great Britain in 1955.

2. _____ Britain's first female prime minister, I served three terms in a row in office. The Soviets nicknamed me the " Iron Lady." My political ideas are called Thatcherism, and they continue to have great influence.

3. _____ Five long years I searched the hot, sandy desert of Egypt in the Valley of the Kings. Finally, in 1922, my search came to an end. I discovered the untouched tomb of the boy king, Tutankhamen.

4. _____ We were known as the Fab Four: John, Paul, George, and Ringo. One of the most famous bands in the history of rock music, we were the first to write our own songs and music. Screaming fans followed us everywhere we performed!

5. _____ I sponsored the first English colony in America. Although my attempts failed twice, I brought potatoes and tobacco back to Britain. As a favorite of the Queen, I was knighted and appointed captain of her guard in 1587.

6. _____ My interest in math, physics, and astronomy led to many contributions to science. Among those contributions were the development of a reflecting telescope, the discovery that white light is made up of the same system of colors seen in a rainbow, and the discovery of gravity.

A. Margaret Thatcher

B. Howard Carter

C. Winston Churchill

D. Sir Walter Raleigh

E. Sir Isaac Newton

F. Beatles

© Carole Marsh/Gallopade International • www.gallopade.com • It's Your World: United Kingdom

Guts and Glory British Style!

A. Nearly 40 percent of the people in England died when this epidemic swept the country. It caused a fever, black spots on the chest, and big black lumps under the arms, on the neck, and at the top of the legs. Most people who got it died screaming in pain within a few days. It was finally discovered that fleas from rats caused the disease.

B. It was built to be a symbol of power, a fortress for defense, and a prison for enemies. The tower is 100 feet tall with walls that are 15 feet thick in places. Many were imprisoned and some had their heads chopped off here. The Garden Tower was also called the Bloody Tower.

C. During his years as king, he had six wives in an attempt to get a male heir to the throne. Two of those wives lost their head—he had it chopped off!

D. He was considered by the Spanish to be a pirate. He plundered Spanish ports in the Caribbean, and brought their treasure home to Elizabeth I. He was the first Englishman to circumnavigate (go all the way around) the globe.

E. In the Whitechapel area of London, 11 women were killed in a series of gruesome murders that took place over three years. Some bodies were found just moments after their murder. The killer was never found, but letters from someone claiming to be the murderer were signed using this alias.

Mixed Up!
Match the paragraph to the word that the paragraph describes.

BLACK PLAGUE ______

JACK THE RIPPER ______

TOWER OF LONDON ______

SIR FRANCIS DRAKE ______

HENRY VIII ______

© Carole Marsh/Gallopade International • www.gallopade.com • It's Your World: United Kingdom

Great Minds Think All the Time!

Sir Isaac Newton was one of the world's greatest scientists! As a young boy, Isaac spent his time making models of things around him, like a windmill or a cart. He made every detail so perfectly that each moving part actually worked! His family owned a farm in England, but Isaac was not interested in farming so he was sent to school at Cambridge University to study.

At Cambridge, Isaac was very interested in science and math. Isaac realized that math could be used to prove his ideas about how the universe works. He studied the work of other scientists, especially Galileo. By combining his ideas with the ideas of other scientists, he was able to discover and prove the rules of motion and gravity.

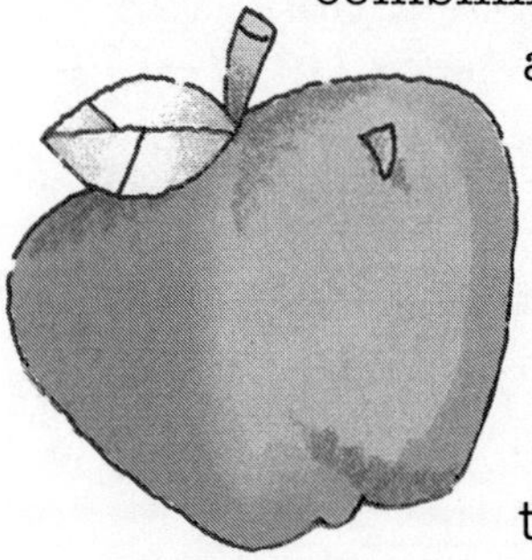

Isaac Newton is probably best-known for his idea of gravity. Watching an apple fall from a tree led him to wonder why the apple falls down to the earth, never up. The answer to that question also explains how the moon is held in its orbit around the earth. Isaac was able to prove that the same rules that apply on earth, also rule the universe. In recognition of his achievements, Isaac was knighted in 1705 and became Sir Isaac Newton!

Colors of the Rainbow!

Isaac Newton used a prism to prove that light was made up of all the colors of the rainbow. Do you remember the acronym for the correct order of the colors in a rainbow? Draw a rainbow below. (Hint: ROYGBIV)

© Carole Marsh/Gallopade International • www.gallopade.com • It's Your World: United Kingdom

King Arthur and Camelot

Have you ever heard of King Arthur and the Knights of the Round Table?

Sir Thomas Malory finished writing the legend of King Arthur in 1470. The story tells about a British king who defends Britain against Saxon invaders.

As the story goes, Arthur, who is heir to the throne, must be raised in a secret place to protect him. When his father dies, there is a dispute about who should rule. The magician, Merlin, sets a sword in a stone. Only the rightful heir to the throne can pull it from the stone. Arthur pulls out the sword and becomes king. He and his knights fight off the Saxons.

Arthur lived in Camelot. At his castle, he and his knights met at the Round Table. They rescued people, fought magical creatures, and searched for the Holy Grail. Arthur had a secret weapon. It was a magical sword called "Excalibur" and he used it against his enemies.

After a period of peace, civil war broke out within the court of Camelot. Arthur was wounded and died. He was put on a boat and floated down river to an island. Three mysterious maidens treated his wounds. His body was never found. Many say that he rests under a hill with all his knights ready to save the country again!

Word play!

The legend of King Arthur lives on. Use the letters in King Arthur's name to create as many words with three letters or more as you can.

KING ARTHUR

© Carole Marsh/Gallopade International • www.gallopade.com • It's Your World: United Kingdom

Big Ben, A Site to See!

The Clock Tower at the Palace of Westminster is home to the world's largest four-faced, chiming clock. It is often referred to as "Big Ben." The name does not refer to the famous tower, or to the four huge clock faces of this landmark; instead, it refers to the largest of the five bells inside the clock tower. It is believed to be called "Big Ben" after Sir Benjamin Hall, the heavy-set Commissioner of Works at the time.

The tower was begun in 1834 following a fire which destroyed the old Palace of Westminster. The clock has become a symbol of the United Kingdom and London. Its chime is used to celebrate both New Year's Day and Remembrance Day in the United Kingdom.

The clock had its first and only major breakdown in August 1976.

There is a light at the top of the tower that, when lit, indicates that the House of Commons is sitting.

The hour bell of Big Ben is 8 feet in diameter and weighs 13.5 tons.

The accuracy of the clock movement is controlled by the placement of old pennies in the mechanism.

The first chime rang on May 31, 1859.

Create your very own travel pamphlet.
Concentrate on an area that interests you. Perhaps you enjoyed learning about the people. Or maybe it was the monuments that interested you. Fold a piece of paper into three sections. This will give you six areas on which to put information.

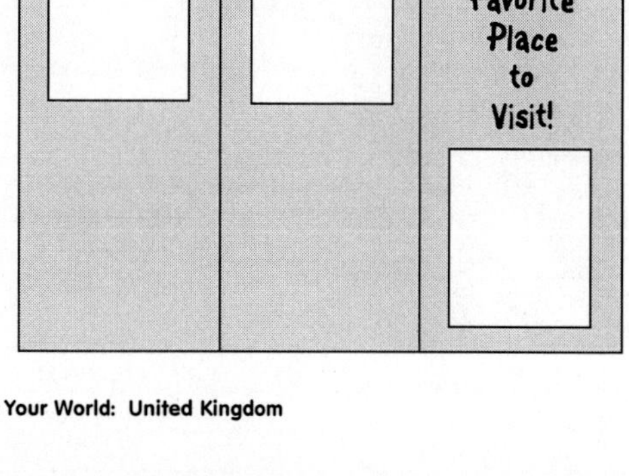

© Carole Marsh/Gallopade International • www.gallopade.com • It's Your World: United Kingdom

It's Customary...

Customs and culture vary widely from country to country. Sometimes they vary in different regions of the same country. Here are custom and cultural differences observed by the British!

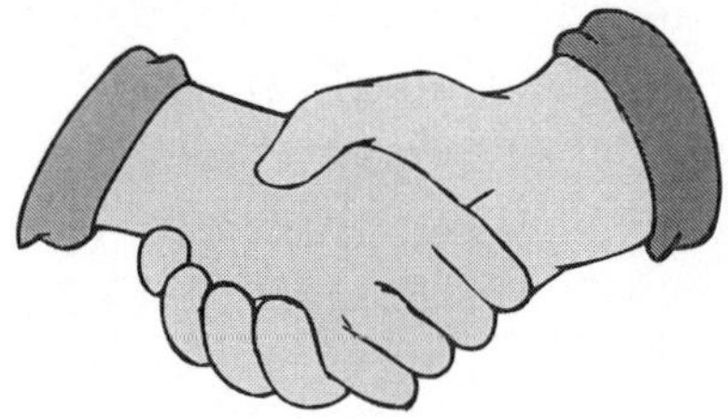

- The handshake is a common greeting.
- When you meet someone and they ask, "How do you do?" the correct response is, "How do you do?"
- Polite manners are very important. It is expected that you say "please" and "thank you."
- Vehicles drive on the left side of the road. That's opposite from the United States!
- It is considered very rude to be late.
- The fork is held in the left hand and the knife in the right. You hold them the opposite way!
- Football is a favorite activity for children in the United Kingdom. We call it soccer!
- The British enjoy gardening. Almost every house has a garden.
- The Spring Bank Holiday is celebrated with a cheese rolling event. Competitors chase a round ball of cheese down a steep hill. This custom is a hazardous one, and many competitors end up with broken bones.

Create your own!

As we have seen, customs and cultural activities can help define who we are. Think about your family and friends and come up with some new customs for everyone to try.

© Carole Marsh/Gallopade International • www.gallopade.com • It's Your World: United Kingdom

What Do They Speak in the United Kingdom?

The official language in United Kingdom is British English. They may speak English, but some of their words are different.

Match it up!
Below are some common British English phrases or words. See if you can match them to the American English word.

British English	American English
Loo	Jello
Biscuit	bathroom
Nappy	guy
Lift	elevator
Torch	cookie
Chips	sweater
Chap	diaper
Jelly	flashlight
Queue	fries
Jumper	line

© Carole Marsh/Gallopade International • www.gallopade.com • It's Your World: United Kingdom

Happy Holidays!

The United Kingdom celebrates many holidays. Some of the celebrations focus on the monarch. In June, the monarch reviews the troops during "Trooping the Color."

Guy Fawkes Day is celebrated on November 5th. Guy Fawkes was a man who tried to blow up the Parliament building in 1605, but failed. The British celebrate this day with fireworks and bonfires. They also set fire to dummies that represent Guy Fawkes. This celebration is also known as "**Bonfire Night**" or "**Mischief Night**" because young people like to play pranks. That sounds like "Trick or Treat," doesn't it?

Christians in the U.K. celebrate traditional Christian holidays, such as **Good Friday**, **Easter Sunday**, and **Christmas**. During Christmas, people exchange cards and gifts. A fun tradition is to pull Christmas crackers. A cracker is a cardboard tube wrapped in brightly colored paper with a surprise inside. When it is pulled by two people, it makes a small bang. The person with the larger half wins the prize!

On Christmas Day, children in the United Kingdom receive gifts from Santa Claus. Write a letter to tell him what you want.

© Carole Marsh/Gallopade International • www.gallopade.com • It's Your World: United Kingdom

United Kingdom Between the Pages and on the Stage

The United Kingdom has a deep culture of literature, music, and theater. It is the birthplace of William Shakespeare, Peter Pan, the Beatles, and Andrew Lloyd Webber.

2.

Notes

1. Some of the world's most beloved children's book characters come from the U.K. like Peter Pan and Harry Potter.

2. Andrew Lloyd Webber turned *The Phantom of the Opera*, a novel by Gaston Leroux, into a world-famous musical.

3. Bagpipes are an integral part of Scotland's culture. They can be heard at distances up to 10 miles in the Scottish Highlands.

4. John Constable was a Romantic painter who painted many scenes about the power of nature.

5. The Beatles, originally from Liverpool, remain the bestselling band in history!

3.

GO!

1.

5.

4.

© Carole Marsh/Gallopade International • www.gallopade.com • It's Your World: United Kingdom

What's for Dinner?

Traditional English meals are often simple. Meat and potatoes are the main staple of English meals. Americans might have a quick snack in the afternoon. But in England, tea and biscuits (cookies) or scones are enjoyed every day around 4:00. Here are a few things to eat if you visit the United Kingdom!

Yorkshire pudding is a batter cake that is baked in meat fat. It is often served with beef.

Steak and kidney pie is a beef and kidney stew that is topped by a pastry crust.

Shepherd's pie is a casserole made of ground meat and mashed potatoes.

Bangers and mash is a dish of sausage and mashed potatoes.

RECIPE

Always ask an adult for help when cooking!

Treacle Tart

INGREDIENTS

2 unbaked pie crusts
6 tablespoons golden syrup (you may substitute light molasses or honey)
2 ounces fresh white bread crumbs
finely grated rind of 1 lemon
1 teaspoon lemon juice

mmmmmmm...this was good!

DIRECTIONS

Line a pie pan with dough of one unbaked pie crust.
Combine syrup, bread crumbs, lemon rind, and lemon juice in a saucepan.
Heat on low until mixture is just melted.
Pour the syrup mixture into the prepared pie crust.
Cut the remaining crust into long narrow strips.
Arrange the strips in a lattice pattern over the filling.
Bake in oven at 400° F for 25 to 30 minutes or until the pastry is slightly browned.

Makes 8 servings

© Carole Marsh/Gallopade International • www.gallopade.com • It's Your World: United Kingdom

Tennis, Anyone?

The Championships, Wimbledon, is the oldest and most honored tennis tournament in the world! Since 1877, the All England Club has hosted the tournament in the London suburb of Wimbledon. It is the only one of the four Grand Slam tournaments played on grass courts.

Each year, 14 days of competition are scheduled in late June to early July. The highlight, the men's singles, is saved for a Sunday afternoon. The event is full of tradition. There is a strict dress code for players and participants. The royal family is always in attendance. The official food is strawberries and cream. Ball boys and girls train for several months before the tournament! They are 14 or 15 years old.

Figure it out!

Figure out the answers to these questions about Wimbledon.

British player William Renshaw (left) is the record holder for the highest number of tournament victories. He has won seven Wimbledon titles!

1. If the last event of Wimbledon is scheduled for Sunday afternoon and the tournament lasts 14 days in a row, on what day of the week will the tournament begin?

____

2. In 2012, there will be 30,000 seats available at Wimbledon. If all seats are occupied for each of the 14 days of the tournament, how many people could potentially see the tournament?

____

© Carole Marsh/Gallopade International • www.gallopade.com • It's Your World: United Kingdom

Lively London!

Engraving showing Old London Bridge in 1616

For more than 100 years, London was the world's largest city and one of the richest! Romans first established a seaport settlement on the banks of the Thames River and called it Londinium. They built a wall around the city for protection and built the first London Bridge of wood.

By the 1500s, the Romans were gone and the city began to grow. Merchants and workers took advantage of its ideal location for trade. London expanded to three times its original size. Soon it was the largest city in the western world. But it was overcrowded and dirty.

In 1665, the black plague killed much of London's population. The plague was followed by the Great Fire, which burned for three days and destroyed two-thirds of the city. The people of London did not give up! The city was rebuilt and became even larger.

In 1940, tragedy struck the world's largest city. German bombers destroyed 80 percent of the city's buildings in World War II. Again, the strength of the British people allowed her to survive and eventually rebuild again!

Use the columns to list the growth and setback events in London.

Growth	Setback

© Carole Marsh/Gallopade International • www.gallopade.com • It's Your World: United Kingdom

United Kingdom Did It First!

Mr. Watson, Come Here, I Want You!
Alexander Graham Bell and Thomas Watson built the world's first telephone.

Stay On Track!
British inventor and engineer George Stephenson built the first practical railroad locomotive.

Hot or Cold!
The Thermos bottle was invented using the same principles created by Sir James Dewar, who invented a flask to store liquefied gas.

The Man Who Named the Clouds!
In the early 1800s, an English chemist named Luke Howard invented a classification for clouds.

Word Fun!

This is fun to do with someone else. Ask a friend for words to substitute for the blanks in the story. Their word substitutions will have a humorous effect when the resulting story is then read aloud.

I want to be the first person to ______________________ (ACTION VERB)

across ______________________ (COUNTRY)! I've been training for this

since ______________________ (MONTH). I'm in ______________________ (ADJECTIVE) shape.

My ______________________ (ADJECTIVE) adventure will begin on

______________________ (FAVORITE HOLIDAY). I won't be hard to miss,

I'll be the one wearing a ______________________ (COLOR)

______________________ (ARTICLE OF CLOTHING) and a pair of matching

______________________ (FOOTWEAR). My faithful friends,

______________________ (FAMOUS ATHLETE) and

______________________ (CARTOON CHARACTER), will be there to cheer for me.

I'm bringing my ______________________ (NOUN) along for good luck.

I'm confident I'll be the first!

I Feel Better Already!
Scottish research scientist Alexander Fleming discovered one of the most important substances in history—penicillin.

Fore!
Allan Robertson of the famous ball-making family in St Andrews, Scotland, is credited as being the first golf professional.

The Answer Book!
Scotsmen Colin Macfarquhar and Andrew Bell founded the Encyclopedia Britannica in 1768.

© Carole Marsh/Gallopade International • www.gallopade.com • It's Your World: United Kingdom

Stupendous Stonehenge!

Stonehenge

A mysterious circle of massive stones sits in the middle of a barren, windswept plain in England. What is it and why is it there? The answer is....no one knows for sure!

Here's what we do know. More than 5,000 years ago on the Salisbury Plain in England, a ditch was dug with deer antlers and wood. About 1,000 years later, in 2,000 B.C., the inner circle was set up. The blue stones that form the inner circle came from a part of England 240 miles away. Eighty of them, weighing about 4 tons each, were moved over water and land. The outer circle was finished about 500 years later. The giant sarsen stones that make up the outer ring weigh up to 50 tons each and come from 20 miles away!

What was the purpose of this great effort? Many people must have worked together for a very long time to build it. Who were they? How did they move the extremely heavy stones over such long distances?

No one knows the answers. Some people who have studied Stonehenge think that it's an enormous calendar built by the Druids. Others believe it's a temple built by the Beaker Folk. One explanation comes from the legend of King Arthur. Merlin is said to have used his magic to bring the stones from Ireland as a monument. Will you be the one to solve the mystery?

What do you think?

Write down some of your ideas about the purpose of Stonehenge.

____

____

____

____

____

____

© Carole Marsh/Gallopade International • www.gallopade.com • It's Your World: United Kingdom

The Blitz

World War II was a terrible time in Europe. In 1940, the German dictator Adolf Hitler conquered France. Shortly after, the Germans began to bomb London.

From September to May, families in London hid in shelters and subways while bombs shook the city. London was filled with the sound of sirens, bombs, and the screams of injured citizens. There was much confusion as people ran from exploding bombs and burning buildings. This frightening time was called "The Blitz."

An especially destructive raid took place on December 29, 1940. More than 1,000 fires sparked by bombs filled the city. More than 30,000 people were killed and 80 percent of London's homes and buildings were destroyed! British military forces continued to fight alongside the United States and other Allied forces. Germany was finally defeated in 1945. The Americans helped rebuild London and other cities after the war.

People sleeping in subway station during the Blitz

Revealing Answer!

Follow the instructions to reveal the name of the building that survived the raid!

1. Cross off the first and last letters.
2. Cross off any letter "O."
3. Cross off the letter that represents the Roman numeral 10.
4. Cross off the second "E" from the left.
5. Cross off the fifth letter from the right (counting only letters remaining).
6. Cross off the seventh and last letters of the alphabet.

BSXT. ZOPGAOUL'S CZATOHGEXDEBRZAXLB

____

© Carole Marsh/Gallopade International • www.gallopade.com • It's Your World: United Kingdom

We've Had Enough, King John!

For most of England's history, kings ruled the land. There were no parliaments; the king was the law. He could rule and tax any way he pleased. In 1199, a very unpopular man was king. His name was King John.

King John forced people to pay high taxes. He fought with everyone—the nobles, the French, even the Pope! Finally, in 1215, the nobles marched an army to London. They forced John to sign the Magna Carta.

"Magna Carta" is a Latin term that means "the Great Charter." This document limited the king's power. First, it said that the king had to obey the law, just like other people. Second, if the king broke the law, the nobles could put someone else in his place. The nobles also formed a council, which became the model for today's British Parliament.

King John signs the Magna Carta

Cross it off!
Starting with the first letter, cross off every other letter to reveal the name of a cathedral which has a copy of the Magna Carta on display.

W S M A O L K I D S B B M U X R Q Y
K C I A E T E H Q E O D N R P A W L

© Carole Marsh/Gallopade International • www.gallopade.com • It's Your World: United Kingdom

Shakespeare, "The Bard"

Shakespeare

People loved William Shakespeare's plays about English history, kings and queens, battles, heroes, and murder! His comedies (full of funny lines and humor) and tragedies (someone always dies) made him the most popular playwright in London. His plays were performed in London's finest theatre, the Globe.

William Shakespeare went to London to make his fortune in the growing theatre business. The queen loved theatre, and playhouses where performances took place were built all over London. William started out taking care of horses for the people who came to watch the plays. Later, he was a prompter, helping the actors when they forgot their lines on stage. He was even an actor himself at times.

The stories had to be changed often to keep the audiences interested. This is where William found his talent. He could write stories that were more exciting than anything people had heard before! It wasn't easy, though, because in the early days of theatre, plays were written like a long poem.

Shakespeare's nickname was "The Bard." The word "bard" means poet. Shakespeare got his nickname because he is said to be the greatest poet the world has ever known. In his lifetime, Shakespeare wrote 37 plays and 154 sonnets (poems). Many of them are still performed today!

> Did you know?
> In early theatre, women were not allowed to act. Young boys played women's roles.

Figure it out!

Can you finish the names of some of Shakespeare's most popular plays?

1. As You _________ ______
2. Romeo and _______________
3. Ham___ ___ ___
4. Mac___ ___ ___ ___
5. ___ ___ ___ ___ ___ ___ ___ Night
6. The Taming of the ___ ___ ___ ___ ___

© Carole Marsh/Gallopade International • www.gallopade.com • It's Your World: United Kingdom

Scottish Fashions – the Kilt!

Highlander

In Scotland, it's the "skirt" that makes the man! The "skirt" tells who a man is; or at least the family to which he belongs! That "skirt" is called a kilt. The Scottish kilt is made from a plaid patterned fabric, called tartan. Each plaid design was created long ago by a local weaver especially for a family or clan. Only members of that family were allowed to wear the special plaid fabric.

The tradition of wearing a kilt began with the Highland Scots. During the time that England ruled Scotland, the Scottish rebelled by wearing tartan as a symbol of national pride.

The Highland Scots fought the English rule, so the English government began taking away rights. The Dress Act restricted the wearing of Highland clothes—the tartan kilts. Only soldiers were allowed to wear the plaid. By the time the Dress Act was repealed, many of the old traditions had been lost. In spite of attempts to revive the traditions, wearing the plaid was no longer seen as a way of life for the Highlanders. Eventually, the plaid became more of a fashion statement for elite English society.

Dress Up!

Help Christina get dressed for her tour of the United Kingdom! These are some of the clothing styles you might see in the U.K. today. Choose which outfit she'll wear. Color the clothing, and draw a line from the piece of clothing to Christina or cut the clothing out and dress her up!

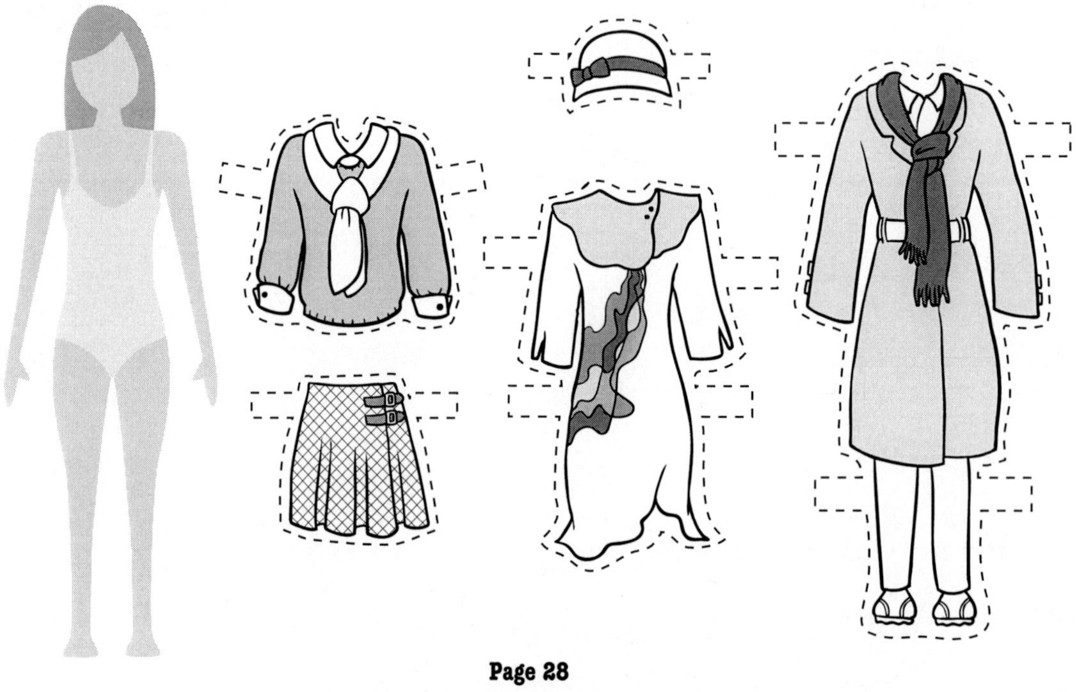

© Carole Marsh/Gallopade International • www.gallopade.com • It's Your World: United Kingdom

Assorted Architecture!

Figure it out!
Use the following clues to figure out the name of this famous building in London, England.

- This church is owned directly by the royal family.
- Since 1066, every monarch of England has been crowned here.
- Until the 19th century, it was the third seat of learning in England, after Oxford and Cambridge.
- Edward the Confessor failed to take a pilgrimage. At the suggestion of the Pope, he built the Abbey to redeem himself.
- The formal name of this building is the Collegiate Church of St. Peter, Westminster.
- English monarchs and other famous people are buried here. Among them are Elizabeth I, Sir Isaac Newton, Geoffrey Chaucer, Charles Darwin, and Charles Dickens.

1. ____

3.

7.

4.

2.

6.

8.

5.

© Carole Marsh/Gallopade International • www.gallopade.com • It's Your World: United Kingdom

As They Say in the United Kingdom...

Very few of the English words of today are English in origin. Here are a few English words that came from other origins:

- **alarm:** a loud signal of warning or danger (from the Italian *all'arme*).
- **assets:** goods or similar advantages, which may be used to obtain or increase money (from the Latin *ad satis*).
- **bribe:** the transfer of goods, money, or services in return for favorable treatment (from the French *brib'er*).
- **cartridge:** a bullet casing, which includes powder and shot as a single unit (from the Middle French *cartouche*).
- **gymnast:** an athlete, who performs gymnastics (from the Greek *gymnastes*).
- **knave (jack):** a scoundrel or thief (from the Old High German *knabo*).
- **manure:** the dung of an animal as used for fertilizer (from the Latin *manu* and *operari*).
- **mile:** a unit of distance consisting of 5,280 feet (from the Latin *milia*).
- **monster:** a beast or creature of terrible or threatening appearance (from the Latin *monstrum*).

Words we use with Irish roots:
- **Smithereens:** "I play the fox"
- **whiskey:** water of life
- **galore:** plenty, enough
- **shanty:** a run-down house
- **spree:** spoils taken in a raid (think cattle)

Words we use with Scottish roots:
- **glamour:** magic, enchantment, and spell
- **gumption:** common sense or shrewdness
- **wee:** small, tiny, minute

Just so you know:

The most commonly encountered Welsh word in English is *penguin*!

© Carole Marsh/Gallopade International • www.gallopade.com • It's Your World: United Kingdom

Further Resources

US Embassy in United Kingdom
24 Grosvenor Square
London, W1A 1AE
United Kingdom
Switchboard: [44] (0)20 7499-9000

United Nations
2 United Nations Plaza
New York, NY 10017

VisitBritain-Britain's National Tourism Agency
Thames Tower
Black's Road
Hammersmith
London
W6 9EL
Phone: 020 8846 9000

British Tourist Authority
www.visitbritain.com

Interesting Websites

http://www.visitlondon.com

http://www.parliament.uk

http://www.irishcultureandcustoms.com/

http://www.scotland.org/

© Carole Marsh/Gallopade International • www.gallopade.com • It's Your World: United Kingdom

Answer Key

Page 7
1. flag 2. queen 3. islands 4. official
5. population 6. United Kingdom

Page 8
1. d 2. d

Page 9

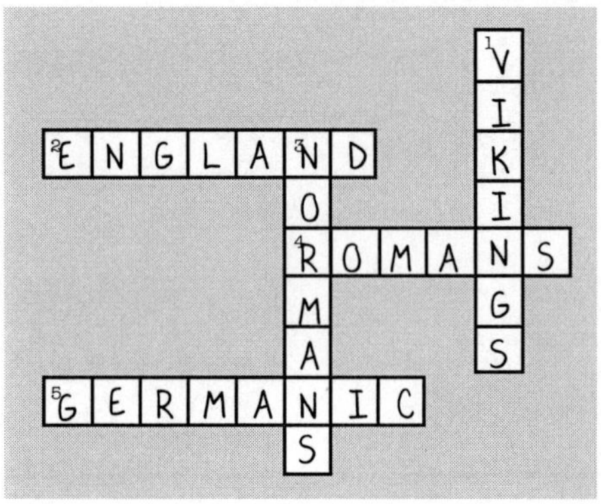

Page 10
4, 1, 6, 3, 5, 2

Page 11
1. c 2. a 3. b 4. f 5. d 6. e

Page 12
Black Plague – A, Jack the Ripper – E,
Tower of London – B, Sir Francis Drake – D,
Henry VIII – C

Page 17

Loo	bathroom
Biscuit	cookie
Nappy	diaper
Lift	elevator
Torch	flashlight
Chips	fries
Chap	guy
Jelly	Jello
Queue	line
Jumper	sweater

Page 21
1. Monday
2. 420,000

Page 25
St. Paul's Cathedral

Page 26
Salisbury Cathedral

Page 27
1. Like It 2. Juliet 3. let 4. Beth 5. Twelfth
6. Shrew

Page 29
Westminster Abbey

© Carole Marsh/Gallopade International • www.gallopade.com • It's Your World: United Kingdom